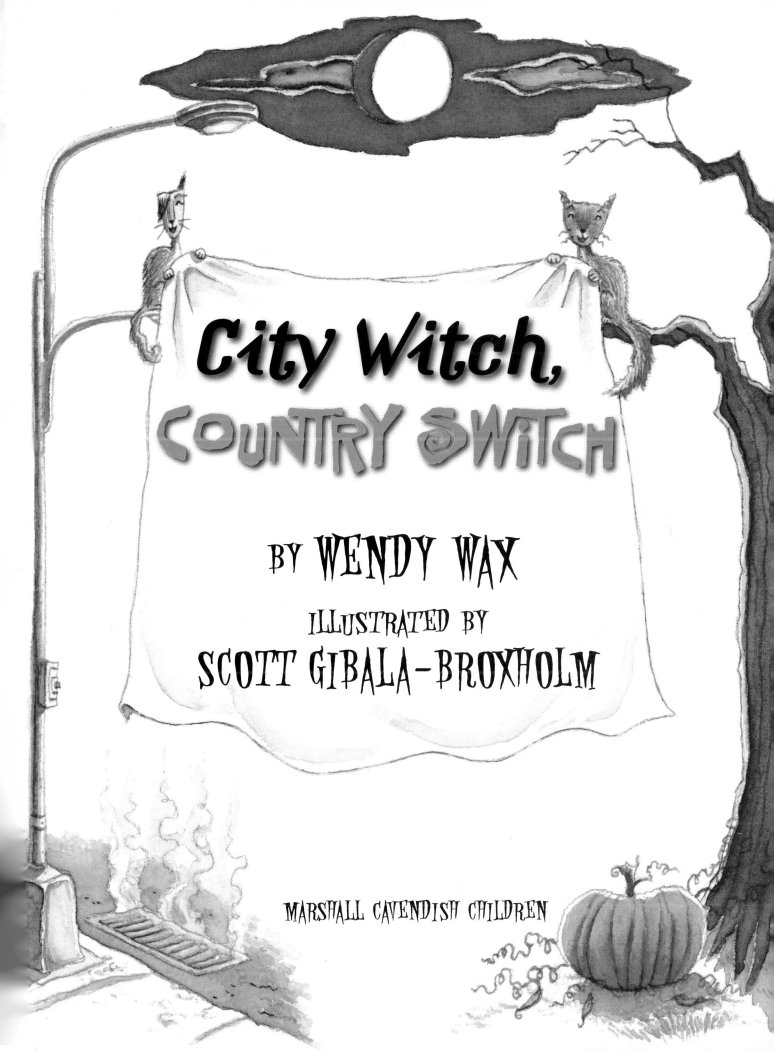

City Witch, COUNTRY SWITCH

BY WENDY WAX

ILLUSTRATED BY
SCOTT GIBALA-BROXHOLM

MARSHALL CAVENDISH CHILDREN

Mitzi was a city witch
who came home late one night
and saw her window open wide.
Had she left on the light?

She soon found that another witch
had landed in her room.
"It's me, your cousin Muffletump!"
her guest squealed. "Wow, nice broom!"

"Muffletump? The country witch?
At last we finally meet!"
The cousins hugged and talked
until the two of them were beat.

That night . . .

Poor Muffletump tossed and turned.
The couch was much too soft.
The street outside was noisy.
She missed her cozy loft.

Remembering a magic spell
to help her fall asleep,
she chanted,

"TWINKLY-WINKLY!"

and . . .

the room filled up
with sheep!

In the morning, Mitzi planned
to show her guest around.
"What dirty air!" groaned Muffletump.
"It's rising from the ground."

She coughed. She sneezed. She chanted,
"PINKA-DINKA-DANDY!"

And suddenly the dirty smoke
turned into cotton candy!

The cousins took a bus uptown
to the museum of art.

"There's hardly room to breathe in here!"
said Muffletump. "STRAW-CART!"

The bus became a hayride,
with seats for everyone.
"Giddyup!" whooped
Muffletump.
"I knew this would be fun!"

"Let's go skating," Mitzi said.
But Muffletump said, "No.
I've had a lot of fun with you,
and now I have to go."

"Bye-bye, noise and smog," she called.
"The country is for me!"
"Wait," yelled Mitzi. "I'll come, too!"
Her cousin whooped, "Yippee!"

They whizzed above the windy sea
as storm clouds settled in.
Muffletump yelled, "DING-DONG!"
while Mitzi shouted, "DIN!"

"BURGER-RIFIC!"

"UPSI-DAISY!"

These ancient words
were all it took
to change the clouds to bells.
After that, they both took turns
casting favorite spells.

When they landed, Mitzi asked,
"You live up in a tree?"
"I sure do!" bragged Muffletump.
"Come in. I'll brew some tea."

This time Mitzi couldn't sleep.
It rained right through the roof!
Night owls hooted, crickets sang,
and Mitzi cried,

Now pitter-patter went the rain,
but Mitzi stayed quite dry,

for a giant pink umbrella soared
above them in the sky.

The next day . . .

"Let's catch some fish," said Muffletump,
"and then we'll take a swim."
Mitzi gasped. "In all this slime . . . ?

SUPER-SUDSY-WHIM!"

Mitzi stripped down to her suit
and jumped in from the path,
for now the pond was bubbly
and perfect for a bath!

Muffletump showed Mitzi
what to pick for Pumpkin Stew.
But Mitzi's only comment was
Ah-choo! Ah-choo! Ah-choo!

"My allergies are acting up," she said,

"TA-MATA-CHEEST!"

The field filled up with pizza~
Mitzi's kind of feast!

"Let's play tag," said Muffletump,
but Mitzi shook her head.
"You are great, but weeds and dirt
are not my style," she said.

"I'll miss you, Mitz," said Muffletump.
Mitzi said, "Me, too."
The witches went their separate ways.
What else could they do?

That evening, both cousins lay awake.
They tossed and turned all night.

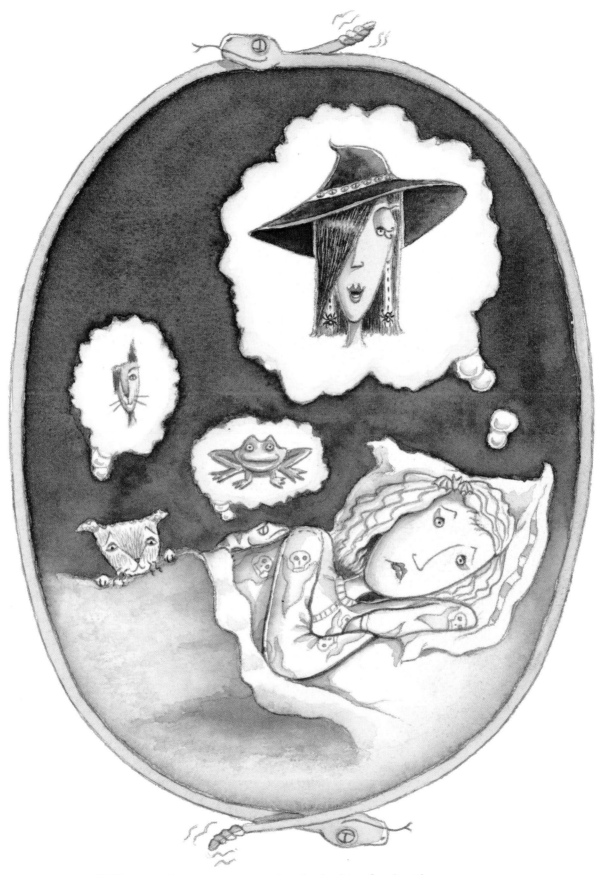

Their homes just didn't feel the same.
Which spell could set things right?

As if they'd read each other's minds, they chanted,

"FAR-NO-MORE!"

When morning came, they waved hello 'cause now they lived next door!

"Howdy, neighbor!" Mitzi said.
Muffletump just smiled. . . .

Then they had a tasty snack, city-country style!

To Mom, who gave me Muffletump; Jon, my beloved cohort,
who conjures supernatural feasts; Nomi, my good-witch,
who forever casts spells of laughter; and Jonah,
my favorite little goblin. —W.W.

With cauldrons full of love to my Aunt Jean,
who has a "magic" all her own! —S.G.B.

Text copyright © 2008 by Wendy Wax. Illustrations copyright © 2008 by Scott Gibala-Broxholm. All rights reserved.
Marshall Cavendish Corporation, 99 White Plains Road, Tarrytown, NY 10591 www.marshallcavendish.us/kids
Library of Congress Cataloging-in-Publication Data Wax, Wendy. City witch, country switch / by Wendy Wax ;
illustrated by Scott Gibala-Broxholm. -- 1st ed. p. cm. Summary: While paying a surprise visit to her city-dwelling cousin,
Muffletump misses her home in the country but when Mitzi leaves the city to see where Muffletump lives, she is just
as uncomfortable until the two, together, conjure a solution. ISBN 978-0-7614-5429-8 [1. Witches--Fiction. 2. Cousins--
Fiction. 3. City and town life--Fiction. 4. Country life--Fiction. 5. Stories in rhyme.] I. Gibala-Broxholm, Scott, ill. II. Title.
PZ8.3.W35Cit 2008 [E]--dc22 2007028855 The text of this book is set in Colwell. The illustrations are rendered in
watercolor washes and colored pencil. Book design by Anahid Hamparian Editor: Robin Benjamin

Printed in Malaysia   1 3 5 6 4 2   First Edition   **mc** Marshall Cavendish Children